Fire Truck Is Flashing

Mandy Archer

Illustrated by Martha Lightfoot

QEB Publishing

The sun rises over the fire station.
Fire Truck waits behind the big red doors.

It is very quiet. Upstairs, the crew is sleeping.

Only Fox keeps one eye open.

The fire alarm starts ringing.

Fox leaps out of bed.

Firefighters rush
to put on **boots**
and zip up **coats**.

Fox is first to **slide**
down the pole.

WHEEEE!

Fire Truck is ready to **go!**

Hurry, **hurry!**

Fox grabs his **helmet** and
climbs into the **driver's cab.**

Fox flicks **switches** and pulls **levers**.

Fire Trucks's motor starts to **rumble** and **shake**.

The fire station doors **spring open.**
Its lights shine **bright.**

VROOM!
VROOM!

Fire Truck **ZOOMS** out.
This is an **emergency!**

Fire Truck **races** through the streets.

Sirens **wail.**
Red lights
flash.

The **Chief** speaks to Fox on the radio.

NEE-NAW!
NEE-NAW!

There's a fire blazing in an apartment building! Fire Truck goes even faster.

Fire Truck **screeches** to a stop
outside the apartment building.

Flames lick the
building and **smoke**
billows out.

Fox quickly **unrolls** Fire Truck's **hose**.

Fox finds a **hydrant** and connects the **hose**.

WWOOOSHH!
A jet of water hits the flames.

The **Chief's** **car** pulls up.

He points to the top floor—
someone is **stuck inside!**

The crew unfolds Fire
Truck's **ladder**.
There's not
a second to lose!

Fox puts on his **mask**
and **air tank**.
The smoke will
make it hard
to breathe.

A woman waves from the top-floor window.

It will be difficult
to reach her.

Fire Truck needs
to move closer.

Fire Truck **edges** back a little bit. The ladder goes **UP** again.

Now Fox can reach!

He carefully **breaks** the **glass** and carries the woman out.

The crowd gives a **big cheer!**

When the last flame has been put out,
the **firefighters** put away their
tools and wind up the hose.

The **fire crew** drives back to the station.
It's been a **busy** day!

HONK! HONK!

Fox is very **proud** of Fire Truck!

Let's look at
Fire Truck

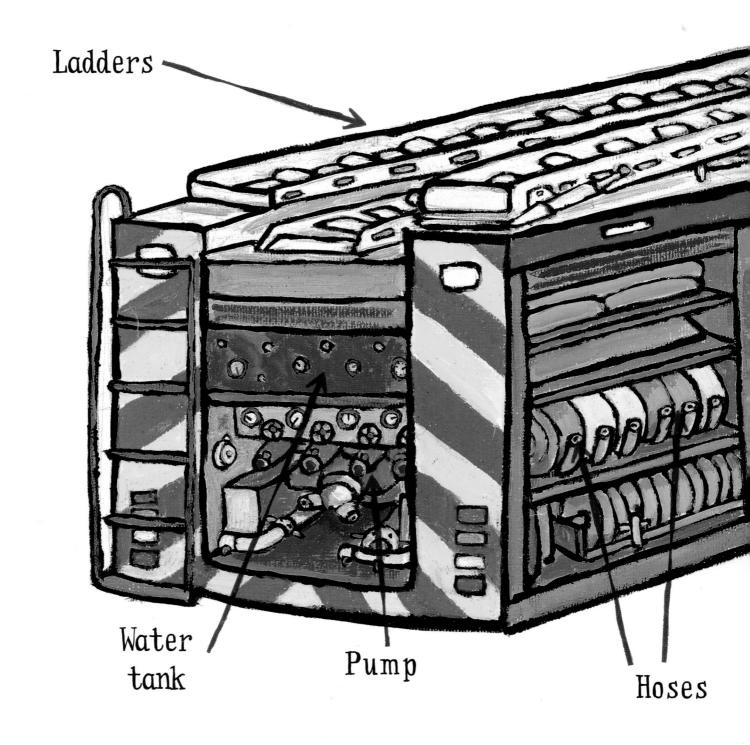

Ladders

Water tank

Pump

Hoses

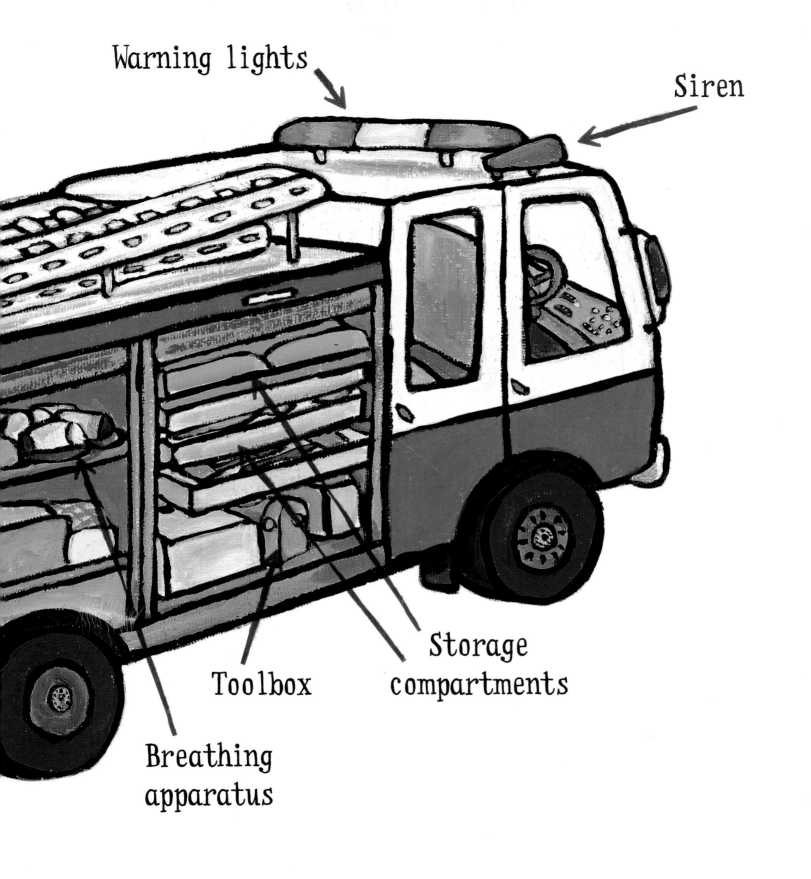

Warning lights

Siren

Toolbox

Storage compartments

Breathing apparatus

Other Emergency Machines

Police car

Emergency helicopter

Ambulance

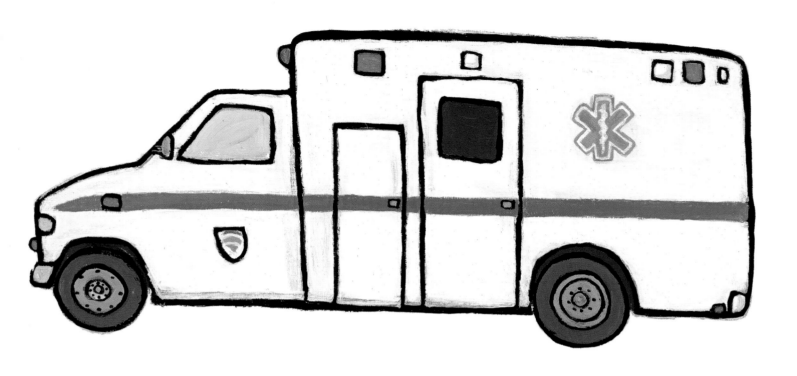

Police motorbike

For Tamar M. L.

Designer: Plum Pudding Design

Copyright © QEB Publishing 2012

First published in the United States in 2012 by
QEB Publishing, Inc.
3 Wrigley, Suite A
Irvine, CA 92618

www.qed-publishing.co.uk

A CIP record for this book is available from the Library of Congress.

ISBN: 978 1 60992 228 3

Printed in the United States